D1507724

A Note to Parents and Caregivers:

Read-it! Readers are for children who are just starting on the amazing road to reading. These beautiful books support both the acquisition of reading skills and the love of books.

The PURPLE LEVEL presents basic topics and objects using high frequency words and simple language patterns.

The RED LEVEL presents familiar topics using common words and repeating sentence patterns.

The BLUE LEVEL presents new ideas using a larger vocabulary and varied sentence structure.

The YELLOW LEVEL presents more challenging ideas, a broad vocabulary, and wide variety in sentence structure.

The GREEN LEVEL presents more complex ideas, an extended vocabulary range, and expanded language structures.

The ORANGE LEVEL presents a wide range of ideas and concepts using challenging vocabulary and complex language structures.

When sharing a book with your child, read in short stretches, pausing often to talk about the pictures. Have your child turn the pages and point to the pictures and familiar words. And be sure to reread favorite stories or parts of stories.

There is no right or wrong way to share books with children. Find time to read with your child, and pass on the legacy of literacy.

Adria F. Klein, Ph.D.
Professor Emeritus
California State University
San Bernardino, California

First American edition published in 2005 by
Picture Window Books
5115 Excelsior Boulevard
Suite 232
Minneapolis, MN 55416
877-845-8392
www.picturewindowbooks.com

First published in Canada in 1999 by
Les éditions Héritage inc.
300 Arran Street, Saint Lambert
Quebec, Canada J4R 1K5

Printed in the United States of America.

Library of Congress Cataloging-in-Publication Data
Tondreau-Levert, Louise, 1949-
When nobody's looking ... / Louise Tondreau-Levert ; [illustrator] Bruno St-Aubin.
p. cm. — (Read-it! readers)
Summary: When their exhausted parents are not looking, the children get into trouble
by playing tricks, having a pillow fight, and misplacing the dog.
ISBN 1-4048-1068-4 (hardcover)
[1. Behavior—Fiction. 2. Family life—Fiction.] I. Title: When nobody is looking.
II. St-Aubin, Bruno, ill. III. Title. IV. Series.

PZ7.T616Wh 2004
[E]—dc22

2004024430

When Nobody's Looking ...

Written by Louise Tondreau-Levert
Illustrated by Bruno St-Aubin

Special thanks to our advisers for their expertise:

Adria F. Klein, Ph.D.
Professor Emeritus, California State University
San Bernardino, California

Susan Kesselring, M.A.
Literacy Educator
Rosemount - Apple Valley - Eagan (Minnesota) School District

PICTURE WINDOW BOOKS
Minneapolis, Minnesota

Jake, the twins, and I are ordinary kids.
You see kids like us everywhere. On Sunday
afternoons, in the park, there are a lot of us.

But when Mom and Dad have their backs turned, what do the kids do?

Like our parents, we like to put things away. To start with, we pick up the chewing gum off the ground and stick it to the park benches. We put on the pink pieces, then the blue, then the yellow, and, finally, the white.

When our parents aren't watching, the twins have face-making contests with the neighbors.

"Trouble! Nothing but trouble!" say
our parents.

We disagree, so we head over to the swings.
Jake and I push the twins. We push them
high—really high!

11

While our parents are talking, we build a huge sand castle. We wrestle to decide who gets to be the king and queen. The sand flies everywhere. We find it in our hair, in our ears, and even in our eyes! By the end we are even eating some!

"Trouble! Nothing but trouble!" grumble our parents.

Mom and Dad take us home right away. We think car rides are fun! We count the cows in the fields, and we sing very loudly.

"Trouble! Nothing but trouble!" grumble our parents.

So that our parents don't have to do the
work, we take the sand out of our shoes in
the car. Then we pull out of our pockets the
little stones and other treasures we found
during the day.

16

Oops! Now the car needs to be washed—
inside and out!

"Trouble! Nothing but trouble!" scold
our parents.

17

Back at the house, Mom and Dad are discouraged and tired.

We try to cheer them up by taking the dog out for a walk.

We accidentally forget to bring Buster back,
and our parents have to look everywhere
for him.

While they are looking, we take care of the
other animals. The twins are sure that the little
black cats would rather be white, so they
decide to give them a bath.

"Trouble, nothing but trouble!" our parents
say angrily.

21

Grandpa invites himself over to dinner. Jake, the twins, and I are thrilled to have him listen to our newest musical number, played on pots and pans.

Despite the noise, Grandpa falls asleep. Jake uses this opportunity to explain to us how Grandpa attaches his suspenders.

"Trouble! Nothing but trouble!" grouch my parents.

Unable to move, Grandpa wakes up in a very, very bad mood.

"That's enough trouble for today! It's time to head to bed!" cry my parents.

Before sleeping, the twins, Jake, and I
need a drink of water, some cookies, a
story, a hug, a little song, a stuffed
animal, a little rhyme, and a last hug.

After that, we have an unforgettable pillow fight. Exhausted, my parents sleep all through the night.

I wonder what we'll do tomorrow?

More *Read-it!* Readers

Bright pictures and fun stories help you practice your reading skills. Look for more books at your level.

A Clown in Love by Mireille Villeneuve
Alex and the Game of the Century by Gilles Tibo
Alex and Toolie by Gilles Tibo
Daddy's an Alien by Bruno St-Aubin
Emily Lee Carole Temblay
Forrest and Freddy by Gilles Tibo
Gabby's School by the Sea by Marie-Danielle Croteau
Grampy's Bad Day by Dominique Demers
John's Day by Marie-Francine Hébert
Peppy, Patch, and the Postman by Marisol Sarrazin
Peppy, Patch, and the Socks by Marisol Sarrazin
The Princess and the Frog by Margaret Nash
Rachel's Adventure Ring by Sylvia Roberge Blanchet
Run! by Sue Ferraby
Sausages! by Anne Adeney
Stickers, Shells, and Snow Globes by Dana Meachen Rau
Theodore the Millipede by Carole Tremblay
The Truth About Hansel and Gretel by Karina Law
When Nobody's Looking ... by Louise Tondreau-Levert

Looking for a specific title or level? A complete list of *Read-it!* Readers is available on our Web site: *www.picturewindowbooks.com*